WARNING

No one is safe from Cupid's dart.
He'll get you straight right through the heart.
Love is blind, but apart from that —
He's a naughty little brat!

PUFFIN BOOKS

Published by the Penguin Group: London, New York, Australia, Canada, India, New Zealand and South Africa

Penguin Books Ltd, Registered Offices: 80 Strand, London WC2R 0RL, England

www.penguin.com

First published by Hamish Hamilton Children's Books 1989
Published by G.P. Putnam's Sons 1990
Published in Puffin Books 2002
Published in this edition 2003
1 3 5 7 9 10 8 6 4 2
Manufactured in China
ISBN 0–241–14212–1

CUPID

Babette Cole

PUFFIN BOOKS

Cupid's mum
was the
Goddess of Beauty.

They lived in the
Land of the Gods.

His mum wanted to win a big beauty prize so they
all took a trip down to earth for the Miss World Competition.

They called themselves Mr and Mrs Jupiter-Jones
and rented a house on Mount Olympus Avenue.

"You'd better behave yourself while we're here, Cupid," said his dad.

"It wouldn't do if they found out we weren't real humans."

"And that means NO FLYING!" said his mum.

But Cupid was a naughty show-off!

He gave the babysitter a bad time!

Then he pinched the little boy
next door's dressing-up outfit!

He soon realised that when he pinged people
with the bow and arrow...

... he could make them fall in love!

Hee hee hee!

He pinged
Miss Bigbody
and Mr Smallbone.

He pinged
Miss Snoutover and
Professor Longbeak!

He pinged Miss Fourfaults
and she got engaged
to her horse!

He pinged the Hi Wun
of Lowhi and he married his elephant!

MISS WORLD BEAUTY COMPETITION

He pinged the judges at
the Miss World Competition.
They all fell in love with
his mum and gave her
first prize!

Some very bad men saw Cupid's picture
in the paper.

FAMOUS COB, FLANAGAN, WINS
IRISH GRAND NATIONAL

MISS WORLD IS A MUM

They snatched Cupid …

… and demanded
a RANSOM!

They locked him up
in a very high tower.

But they didn't realise ...

... Cupid's wings
were real!

He flew over some very fat
ladies doing their open air
keep fit class!

And he pinged them!

They all fell in love with
the very bad men...

... who ran away
and were never seen again.

But Cupid
broke his bow!

Cupid's mum and dad were pleased to get him back.

But he wouldn't stop crying about the bow!

Back in the Land of the Gods
Cupid's dad gave him
an even better bow.

And he's been causing trouble ever since!